With love to Sam and Dorothy Thompson,
whose imagination helped make this book a reality.

And to our family and friends,
who offered advice and guidance.

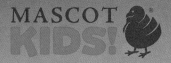

www.mascotbooks.com

Goodness Gracious Golly Gee: I Forgot My Christmas Tree!

For more information, please contact:
Mascot Books
620 Herndon Parkway, Suite 320
Herndon, VA 20170
info@mascotbooks.com

Library of Congress Control Number: 2021908867

CPSIA Code: PRT0821A
ISBN-13: 978-1-64543-535-8

Printed in the United States

Goodness Gracious Golly Gee
I FORGOT MY CHRISTMAS TREE!

Carol & Cori Burcham

Illustrated by Agus Prajogo

I imagined what could be,
If Santa saw what I could see...

Goodness gracious golly gee,
I forgot my Christmas tree!
Goodness gracious golly gee,
What will Santa think of me?

There's no place for the toys to be put
When he arrives down the chimney in soot.
Appearing before my living room,
Santa will tumble in with a boom!
With no decorations to be had,
Oh, how he will feel so sad!

Goodness gracious golly, oh my!
I forgot to bake the Christmas pie.
Goodness gracious golly, oh my!
Santa will let out a great big sigh.

A single tear will fall from his eye
When he sees there's no Christmas pie.
With his tummy a-rumbling, he'll cry,

"Where are my cookies and
where's my milk?"
Then I'll think to myself,
"Oh, I feel so much guilt!"

Goodness gracious golly gee,
What is the matter with me?
Goodness gracious golly gee,
I messed up so epically!

Where's the garland, stockings, mistletoe, and more?
For soon, Santa will burst through that door.
He'll burst in bellowing, "Ho, Ho, Ho!"
Oh, there's so much to do. I better go!

Goodness gracious golly gee,
It's already a quarter to three!
Goodness gracious golly gee,
There's no way! It can't be!

Hope this is a nightmare—
Wake me up with a pinch,
For Santa will mistake me
for a grinch!
He'll think I have no
Christmas cheer,
When, really, it's just that
I forgot this year.

I'll swish through the door,
As quick as a flash,
And run to my car—
I hope I have cash.

I'll get to the mall;
It's not very far.
They'll have it all—
 Alex's book and Ryan's guitar.

But wait, can it be?
Is that reindeer I see?
On top of my roof!
Oh, good golly gee!

I adjust my specs
To get a better look.
Not what I'd expect,
Like out of a storybook.

I see Dasher, Dancer, Prancer, and Vixen,
And sliding down into the snow was Blitzen!
He said to me, "Sir, how do you do?"
And I said in a huff, "Oh, I feel so blue!"

"I've ruined Christmas!
I've turned it to poo!"
"You haven't ruined Christmas!
Let me give you a clue...

Christmas isn't about presents and goodies galore!
It's about family, love, and so much more!
You see, Santa won't be mad if there's no tree,
As long as there's cheer, he'll be happy as can be!"

Then he raised his hoof,
Pointing it to the window.
Inside were elves
All playing limbo!

He said, "Join the celebration!
Throw away your frustration!
Don't you dare shed a tear!
You'll do better next year!"

Goodness gracious golly gee,
Look what the elves have done for me!
Goodness gracious golly gee,
Blitzen, look what's in front of me!

Presents, stockings, decorations, lights,
Mistletoe, holly, would have been a delight!
Instead, I join my family by the fire.
This is all I really desire!

No presents were needed
To make them smile.
Family and love
Was here all the while!

Goodness gracious golly gee,
I never really needed the tree!
Goodness gracious golly gee,
Christmas magic is all around me!

Inspired by our dog Beau

ABOUT THE AUTHORS

Carol and Cori Burcham are a mother-daughter writing team from northern Delaware, who love whimsical stories that foster a child's imagination and curiosity. Their first children's book is based on a rhyme composed by Carol's father.

After teaching kindergarten and first grade for fourteen years, Carol was inspired to write her own children's book after reading picture books in her classes from her favorite authors, Eric Carle and Jan Brett. She graduated from the University of Delaware with a degree in Early Childhood Education. While working full-time and raising three children, Carol also took graduate-level courses to advance her degree.

Cori is an aspiring novelist and a graduate from the University of Delaware with a degree in English with a concentration in Creative Writing. Cori's short story "The Pocket Watch" is published in the University of Delaware's literary magazine, *Caesura*. She wrote two comic books for the education initiative known as "The Ese'Eja Graphic Novel Project." She is currently a freelance journalist.

GOODNESSGRACIOUSGOLLYGEE.COM